I0669841

J. Lansing (John Lansing) Burrows

The Christian Scholar and Soldier. Memoirs of Lewis Minor

Coleman

J. Lansing (John Lansing) Burrows

The Christian Scholar and Soldier. Memoirs of Lewis Minor Coleman

ISBN/EAN: 9783337136741

Printed in Europe, USA, Canada, Australia, Japan

Cover: Foto ©Raphael Reischuk / pixelio.de

More available books at **www.hansebooks.com**

VIRGINIA BAPTIST SUNDAY SCHOOL AND PUBLICATION }
BOARD, *Richmond.* } No. 109.

THE

CHRISTIAN SCHOLAR AND SOLDIER.

MEMOIRS

OF.

LEWIS MINOR COLEMAN,

PROFESSOR IN THE UNIVERSITY OF VIRGINIA—LIEUT. COL. OF
FIRST REGIMENT VIRGINIA ARTILLERY.

BY J. L. BURROWS, D. D.

RICHMOND:
CAY & CO. PRINTERS,

CHRISTIAN SCHOLAR AND SOLDIER.

BY J. L. BURROWS, D. D.

In the history of the Church are to be found recorded, in each generation, the names of a few disciples of Jesus, who have manifestly and practically subordinated all earthly interests to the higher claims of piety. Not in indefinite theory, which all accept, but by spirit and life, they have revealed to the world, that they were seeking " first the kingdom of God and His righteousness." They have " let their light so shine before men, that the world has seen their good works and glorified the Father in Heaven." While " diligent in business, they have been fervent in spirit, serving the Lord."

This class of Christians—always, alas! too few in number—may prosecute with diligence and earnestness their honest secular business, perform promptly and faithfully every worldly duty, but they evince, so that it becomes recognized by all familar with them, that the spirit of consecration to Christ Jesus, overrides all other interests. They are " always ready to every good work."

Industrious as artizans, earnest as Christians; effective as merchants, devout as disciples of Jesus; thorough and enthusiastic as students of worldly lore, most learned in the word of God; brave and enduring as soldiers fighting for homes and liberties, bolder and firmer as soldiers marshalled under the banner of Chri

Such in humble life was John Pounds, the crippled cobbler of Portsmouth, England, who made his shop, six feet by eighteen, a school-room, and hired, with roast potatoes, " the little blackguards," as he called them, of the docks and hovels, to come to him and sit by his stall while he worked, and be taught how to read, right and cypher; thus gratuitously establishing the first " ragged school."

Such was Harlan Page, a carpenter, who respectfully and tenderly, either in personal conversation or by letter, addressed every person to whom he could with propriety gain access, upon the claims of Jesus and the necessity of a pious life.

Such a consecrated life was that of Samuel Budgett, whose first trade was with a horse shoe, picked up in the road, carried three miles and sold for a penny, and who gradually worked himself by energy and industry, into the front rank of princely English merchants, scattering munificent Christian charities all along his pathway, maintaining an humble, devout and benevolent heart, and declaring when on his death bed,—" Riches I have had as much as my heart could desire, but I never felt any pleasure in them for their own sake, only so far as they enabled me to give pleasure to others."

Such was Nathaniel Ripley Cobb, who at twenty-three years of age, upon entering business, solemnly " Resolved by the grace of God never to be worth more than $50,000;" and who, when his fortune reached that point, notwithstanding great liberality in his charities meanwhile, conscientiously gave away to benevolent purposes the whole accumulating surplus, evincing, all the while, a personal devotedness that improved all opportunities for doing good, and who died at the age of thirty-six, directing that his epitaph should be " Christ is my hope."

Such a Christian was our own James C. Crane, whose life was consecrated first to Christ and His cause, and who suffered no business engagements, however pressing or promising profit, to interfere with his religious duties.

Such a Christian, as a student and a philosopher, was Sir Isaac Newton, whose profoundest researches, passing beyond the measurement and weighing of stars, demonstrated the truth and preciousness of God's word, and who, when dying, joyfully anticipated exploring the treasures of the immense ocean of truth, upon the pebbled shore of which he deemed that he had only been playing as a child.

As soldiers, this spirit of consecration has produced such men as Colonel Gardiner and Headly, Vickars and Havelock, whose pious influence over his regiment procured for them the play-soubriquet of "Havelock's Saints"—and our own Jackson—the most eminent trait of whose character was not courage, nor genius, nor energy, nor endurance, conspicuous as these were, but simple and earnest piety.

Such a Christian, too, in his sphere, as a scholar and a soldier, was LEWIS MINOR COLEMAN, a grateful tribute to whose memory, as one of our own young men, we propose in this little tract to furnish,

Lewis M. Coleman was born in Hanover county, Va., February 3d, 1827. His father, Thomas B. Coleman, was a prominent and honored citizen of Caroline county, connected with its most influential families, and for several years its representative in the Virginia Assembly. He died in the prime of life and while his children were yet very young. His mother, Mary O. Coleman, was the daughter of Robert Coleman, of Hanover county, a gentleman highly esteemed for his probity and benevolence. After the death of her first husband, Mrs. Coleman returned to Chantilly, her father's home, always the abode of refinement and hospitality, and subsequently married Dr. George Fleming.

As a boy, Lewis was thoughtful, affectionate and

studious. From childhood he cherished reverence and love for his parents, which manifested itself in uniform and unquestioning obedience, and in anxiety to please them and gain their approval. As the elder brother in the family, he was devoted and faithful, reproving earnestly what he deemed errors and faults, yet in such a spirit of tenderness and affection as ever to knit more closely the bands of love that united them.

In promoting the happiness of a growing family much depends upon the character and spirit of the eldest child, who is the more immediate pattern to the younger, with whom they are more closely associated, and whose temper and habits are, of necessity, most directly watched and imitated. It has been remarked, that boys reared in companionship with a loving and cultivated elder sister are likely to be more gentle, unselfish and affectionate, more free from rude and boisterous habits, than others. Favorable results necessarily follow such sweet moulding control. Young Coleman seems to have exerted over the younger members of the rising family an influence somewhat akin to a sister's in its tenderness, yet manly in its tendencies to honor, truthfulness and self-reliance.

The life and character of Lewis Minor Coleman furnishes another illustration to the long catalogue, exhibiting the influence of a pious mother's training. What St. Paul averred concerning young Timothy might be appropriately said of him, "the unfeigned faith that is in thee dwelt first in thy grandmother Lois, and in thy mother Eunice." He often said that whatever of good there was in his nature or life he owed to his mother. She exerted a vigorous and practical, yet loving influence in training her children, not weakly shrinking from chastisement; prompt, firm and unalterable in her decisions, yet so manifestly just and affectionate as to win confidence, respect and love. The mothers most slighted, least respected by children when grown, are just those who have been most weakly indulgent, who have restrained and controlled their children least when they were young.

A little incident will illustrate both the discipline of the mother and the marked character of the boy. The two elder brothers, much alike as to size and dress, had been set to some light task in the yard. Upon some sudden boyish quarrel the younger struck Lewis a blow, under which he fell to the ground. Just passing the window, the mother caught a glimpse of the fray, and hastening towards them, found the younger prostrate upon the ground, where he had thrown himself in his excitement, and in order to deceive the coming mother into the belief that he was the injured party, and Lewis standing in a threatening posture over him. Taking it for granted that the blow had been given by Lewis, she took him by the arm, broke a switch from a convenient lilac bush, and punished him He simply said, " Mother, I did not strike him." Supposing she could trust her own eyes, she whipped him again for telling a falsehood, and yet once more for persisting in it. He brought no accusation against his brother—never reproached him for the blow, nor for his silence in permitting him to receive an unjust chastisement, and, without any allusion to the circumstance, he resumed at once his ordinary pleasant intercourse.

Years passed, and both were grown. One day, in speaking of Lewis, then absent, the mother observed, "I never knew him to tell a falsehood, or even to prevaricate, but once, and for that I never could account." " Mother," said the brother, " that matter has troubled my conscience for a long time. Your eyes deceived you. I struck the blow you saw given. and Lewis told the truth." "Big as you are," replied the mother, " I have a great mind to whip you for it now "

His mother was literally and practically the early educator of her children. She directed their studies and heard their daily recitations. When, at eleven or twelve years of age, Lewis graduated from this home school and entered the more public school at Colonel Fontaine's, in Hanover county he was pronounced the best prepared boy at the school. He frequently said that whatever proficiency he had attained as a student was attributable to the thorough grounding in primary studies, and the right habits of accurate study, imparted by his mother's teachings.

A passing hint is here suggested which young mothers may profitably ponder.

One who was intimately associated with him in childhood, youth and manhood, at the academy and the University, his room-mate at both, and his trusted friend till death, Major Charles Morris, to whom I am indebted for many of these interesting reminiscences, says of him: "My earliest distinct recollection of him was as a boy of seven or eight years old. I remember him as sprightly and joyous, and, even then, to my boyish recollection, evincing those amiable and winning traits toward his companions which eminently distinguished him through life. I remember that then he was far beyond boys of his age (he was nearly a year younger than myself) in information, and distinctly recall a pang of envy that I felt at seeing him open an atlas and speak familiarly of places upon it of which I knew nothing till years after, and of his being held up as a boy for me to emulate. I believe that this, perhaps, was the commencement of a friendly emulation which never ceased during our whole school and college life, but which never ruffled our intimacy or did aught but service to both."

In 1841 young Coleman entered Concord Academy. In Caroline county, a school of which his distinguished uncle, Frederick W Coleman, afterwards for several years a prominent member of the Virginia Senate, was proprietor and principal, and which was regarded as one of the most thorough and effective institutions of its class in the Southern country. It is the concurrent testimony of his associates that he was admired and loved by all his companions, and, what can rarely be said of any youth, was at the same time plainly the favorite of the teacher and yet the favorite of the students. Cheerful, sprightly, jocund in his intercourse with his fellows, ready and eager in all youthful sports, he was yet so manly, truthful and prudent that he excited no enmities and compelled respect and deference.

Petulant and ill-natured criticism of officials and superiors is a weakness of human nature, developed not only in time of war, and by editors and grumblers, who would be men of stupendous intellect and influence if their wisdom only equalled their self-conceit, but it is a weakness incident, as we know, to student life. Indeed, it is not unlikely, could we trace out the biographies of men, that we should find that the carpers and snarlers of the press, the bar-room and street corners, were the carpers and snarlers of the academy and college. One of the boys at Concord Academy, irritated by some fancied grievance from the teacher, was abusing him roundly to a gathered group of boys and relieving his spleen by calling him "Old Fred," when, glancing behind him he saw Lewis Minor gravely standing within ear-shot. He immediately turned to him with a frank apology for what he had said, assuring him that he meant no harm and begged him to forget it. Now, a little incident of this sort shows the estimate of his character, and the regard for his feelings formed by his companions, of whom he was among the youngest. It was a spontaneous testimony of the respect which he personally inspired.

In industry and thoroughness of preparation for recitations he stood first in all his classes. Especially did he excel in acquiring languages. At the same time he pursued quite an extensive course of general reading, which his tenacious and accurate memory so arranged among its stores as to have ever ready for prompt use. He did not confine his studies to the prescribed curriculum. "He proposed to me," says Major Morris, "and in spite, of many short-comings on my part, persistently carried out his plan, that we should read together in our leisure hour all the plays of Sophocles, so as to gain so much advantage when we should enter the University. Often since have I had cause to thank him for his well-timed diligence."

A lad of fourteen, who can thus impose upon himself extra studies, and perseveringly prosecute them while at school, will be likely to leave his mark upon the world.

Always cheerful and sprightly, ready for any innocent sport, he still maintained an unspotted moral reputation, steadfastly resisting all allurements to youthful vices, and exhibiting a strict integrity and manly sense of honor, evincing that even then his actions were controlled by fixed principles, deliberately formed, and from which by no temptations could he be swerved. A naturally quick temper he had already learned to keep under control, so that one of his classmates avers : "I never knew him to have a quarrel." In religious services he was always reverential and attentive, exhibiting thus early that veneration for truths divine which ripened into a most lovely and devout Christian character and life. Of this part of his life his school-fellows still speak with enthusiastic admiration, and there were formed friendships which were interrupted only by death.

In 1844, when about seventeen years old, Lewis entered the University of Virginia. With the tearful and prayerful blessing of his mother, as she parted from him, wringing tears from his own eyes, he passed out to the carriage that was to bear him away. His aged grandfather, with his old-world ideas of the dissipations and frolic abandon of college life, followed him out and, taking him by the hand, said: " My son, don't drink too much, and be sure to pay your debts, or let me know and I will pay them for you." With a cheerful smile, he readily promised to duly regard the old gentleman's warning, and as they rode away said to his companion, " Grandpa seems to have fears concerning me which mother has not; I hope she knows me best." The result proved that the mother's instinctive knowledge of the heart of her boy was truest.

His room-mate and class-mate while at the University thus writes of this part of his life: " He took his usual high stand in the classes and among the students. His reputation as a student and scholar had preceded him, and his actual merits showed not undeservedly. Here, again, he met with many of his old schoolmates. All the beautiful traits of his boyhood were deepened and intensified. Keeping steadily before him the objects he had in view, through a University education he permitted none of the allurements of student life to wile him from his persevering pursuit of learning. His strong and inborn sense of right and honor, and the ever remembered admonitions of his mother, held him aloof from all the dissipations and vices of college life. And yet none was more ready than he to take part in all innocent and cheerful social enjoyments. No one was more sought out by the quiet and studious members of the University, at their social gatherings, where his gaiety, brilliancy and wit were always the life of the party. His progress in the studies of the school was rapid and thorough. Gaining the highest reputation for scholarship, he passed through the difficult curriculum of the University course in two years."

It is understood that the student who after a two years course applies for the degree of Master of Arts at the University of Virginia will likely be subjected to a most rigorous examination, that will be fitted to humble his presumption if not thoroughly prepared. Triumphantly he passed through this ordeal, graduating in every school with honor, and, with the loving benediction of his Alma Mater, received the highest honors she bestows, before he was nineteen years old.

And now in what direction will this youthful graduate turn his first thoughts? Elated by his successes and honors, flattered and caressed by his friends, with a brilliant future opening before him, will he deem life's work accomplished, throw off the restraints of modesty and integrity, and become proud, wilful, self-reliant and reckless. Let us see. Returning to Chantilly, it was observed that he seemed serious and depressed. So painful a contrast did this mood present to his uniform buoyant cheerfulness, that his watchful mother feared that some concealed fault or misfortune was distressing his soul. He courted solitude; spent much time alone. At length she ventured to inquire what caused him so much evident anxiety and distress. He answered her, that he felt himself to be a great sinner against God's laws; that although he had from childhood received and enjoyed the richest bounties of Providence, he had cherished an ungrateful and impenitent spirit; that while nothing he could wish for had been withheld from him, while blessings infinitely more precious than he had deserved, or could have dared to ask, had been lavished upon him, all these blessings he had selfishly appropriated to his own enjoyment and desire for worldly distinction, while all the time he had been guiltily unmindful of the beneficent God who had bestowed them. He exhibited profound distress and self-abhorrence that he had lived so long unreconciled to God, unwon by the grace and love of Jesus the Saviour. He earnestly expressed his purpose to consecrate his heart and life to the service of God, to make His word his study, that he might understand His will, and to bring his spirit and conduct into conformity with its precepts. In his peculiarly brilliant and felicitous conversational manner he would expatiate on the wonders and beauties of God's Holy word, which, though he had read it from childhood, seemed now to open upon his mind as freshly and forcibly as a new revelation. With a deeper interest than he had ever taken in his ordinary studies because he felt that his eternal well-being and happiness were involved in his researches, he entered upon the study of the Book of God, until, satisfied of its truth and divine inspiration, he joyfully yielded his soul to the method of salvation through the Mediator which it revealed, took into his heart its precious promises, and solemnly resolved to subject his soul and life to its commandments.

Here he passed through that marvellous internal change which the Scriptures call being "born again," "created anew in Christ Jesus," and which transforms its subject from a carnal to a spiritual man. He now saw that life had other and nobler ends than he had hitherto proposed to himself, and with the decision that always characterized his nature, without weak procrastination, he formally and solemnly consecrated soul and body to the service of that Jesus who had died for him. This is what he did!

And is there not something morally sublime in this deliberate choice? Just now, while life was opening beautiful vistas before his imagination, triumphs and honors in the past pointing forward to triumphs and honors in the future, while the world was luring him to its pleasures and rewards, he renounces that world as his portion and joy, and solemnly and deliberately devotes himself to a self-denying life for other's good and for God's glory. Here is an example for young men, standing yet upon the threshold of home, looking out, and about to leap into the arena of business strife, which we may well commend to their consideration.

About this time Lewis visited Richmond with his parents. On the evening of the weekly lecture at the First Baptist Church he left a circle of young companions, somewhat chagrined by his withdrawal from the gay gathering, and, without any intimation of his purpose, accompanied his father and the elder members of the family to the lecture. At the close of the service he modestly expressed his desire to unite with the Church, and to receive the ordinance of baptism. Giving clear evidence of the renewing work of God's Spirit upon his heart he was received into the fellowship of the Church, and the next evening, November 12th, 1846, he was solemnly baptised by Rev Mr. Jeter. He had not yet reached the twentieth year of his age. Thus early he brought the honors he had won, the endowments with which he was so liberally gifted, the anticipations of the future opening so brightly before him, and laid all humbly at the foot of Christ's Cross. A most appropriate and auspicious hour was this when just about selecting his profession for life, and entering upon its active duties, he publicly avouched his faith in Jesus and united himself in solemn covenant with His disciples.

Here is a pattern worthy of being copied by our young men. How many, who have disappointed the hopes which fine talents and careful culture have raised, would have been saved a useless, injurious, wretched life, an early and hopeless death, by thus sincerely and intelligently dedicating their youth to God, and throwing around themselves the encouragements and restraints of a religious profession.

Having deliberately devoted his life to the profession of teaching, young Coleman accepted the invitation of his uncle, Mr. F. W Coleman, and became his assistant in Concord Academy.

"The difficulties," says one of his friends, "which surround an assistant teacher in a large public school, are well known and have been often sketched. It is rare that a subordinate can even obtain the respect of the pupils, or that controlling influence over them which will enable him to command obedience and attention. To this difficult task he was found fully equal. He was universally popular with the students. He here commenced to develop that wonderful faculty of controlling boys which so eminently distinguished him in after life."

After a few years the Concord Academy was closed, and Mr. Coleman established the Hanover Academy, near Taylorsville. This was one of those admirable country boarding-schools, where, removed from the enticements and corruptions of the city, young men gathered into a rural home, forming a family, of which the Principal is the head, lay in mental culture, the basis of future enjoyment and usefulness. Under the management of Mr. Coleman, the Hanover Academy was among the first of its noble class.

His reputation for scholarship, his pure personal character, his previous experience at Concord, and the popularity he had acquired among the students, combined to ensure success from the commencement.

His school was uniformly filled with students to the utmost capacity of its gradually enlarging accommodations. They came from all sections of our southern country, and applications were more numerous than places. His labors were very arduous.

He neglected, he postponed no present duty. Visitors most welcome, friends most beloved, while tarrying under his roof, could not detain him from the ordinary drudging duties of his profession. From the most genial and interesting society he would tear himself away to correct exercises or to attend to the petty details of business, saying, with a pleasant smile, "you must excuse me; but I must tramp on the tread mill."

Rev. Dr. Taylor, for several years his pastor, says: "He possessed a wonderful administrative talent in the management of his school. With from sixty to a hundred young men under his care, all to teach and feed and lodge, he so arranged as to give general satisfaction in these different departments, and with remarkable judgment and self-possession. He never seemed in a hurry. He was an admirable disciplinarian. The vicious he knew how to restrain and punish with rigor and firmness, while the inconsiderate and erring he knew how to admonish and influence for good."

His students were found upon examination thoroughly prepared for the University course and took high rank in that institution. He thus, too, in connection with worthy cotemporaneous teachers, contributed much to elevate the grade of schorlarship in the University itself, and to secure for it that high degree of popularity which drew a larger number of students to its halls than to any other college on this continent.

All who had opportunities for judging, speak in highest terms of the management and discipline of the school. He established in all things inexorable system and regularity, and while decided, prompt and firm, he was yet so just, impartial and kind in all, that he won the pupils to confidence and affection for him. He made them feel that he was their friend, and they sought his counsel as though he were an

elder brother, and few left his roof who did not remain in after life his enthusiastic admirers and firm
friends. "The young men under his care," says Dr
Taylor, "regarded him with respect and admiration
as a scholar, and many of them loved him as a brother. Having met with many of them while under his
tuition and afterwards, I do not remember, in a single
instance, to have heard him spoken of in disparag-
ing terms, while many bore willing testimony to his
integrity and worth as a man and to his ability as a
teacher. Nor was this all. They respected him as
an earnest Christian. He was never ashamed of his
religion."

He never entered upon the duties of the day without earnest prayer to God. Daily he gathered his
pupils about the family altar, read with them the
word of God and offered for them fervent supplica-
tions to the Father of all. On Sabbath morning they
regularly met as a Bible class, of which he was the
interested and instructive teacher. When kept from
the sanctuary, he conducted public worship with
them, frequently reading to them a well selected ser-
mon.

Under such pious influence, it seems perfectly natural that Dr. Taylor should say of his pupils, "I
never knew a more respectful class of hearers. Their
regard for him, as well as their own sense of propriety thus educated, induced a general demeanor in
the house of God so marked in its decorum as to
secure the observation of all." He employed too, by
his liberal expenditures, the neighboring pastors, of
different denominations, to preach to the students,
and by all means within his reach strove to promote
their spiritual culture.

One who, better than any other, became familiar
with his inner life, the loving wife, to whom he was
married while at the Academy, says : "During the
last four years of his stay at Hanover Academy, he

became daily more assiduous in his labors, indeed a slave to the high principles of duty that actuated him at all times." While he often deplored the necessity which required so much of his time "in the tread mill exercises of his daily routine," yet he never spared himself a step upon that tread mill. He longed for leisure and opportunity to cultivate and store his mind in more enlarged and congenial studies, yet he never postponed a present practical duty to this longing. Most of all did he lament that his pressing occupations prevented his fuller and more direct consecration to the service of God. "God knows," said he, " I try to do good, and sometimes trust and believe that there are those whose hearts and lives will be improved by my teachings, and whose aspirations will be excited for high and holy endeavors." Sometimes, in despairing mood, he would mourn that he did so little in God's service, and regret that he had not become one, though even among the humblest, of the ministers of Christ's gospel. Yet ordinarily he was cheerful, buoyant, even gay in the discharge of his duties. Capable of instantly concentrating all his powers upon the present mental labor, with equal facility he could throw off the burden and seem in his hours of relaxation as free of care and anxiety as a child. In his chamber, playing with his children, walking about the premises, superintending the farming operations, riding alone along the road, it became a habit in low undertone to warble or to whistle, not "for lack of thought," but as an accompaniment to thoughts, and occasionally to break out aloud in the words of some favorite hymn, such as "Jesus, I love Thy charming name," or " Rock of ages cleft for me." There was nothing of asceticism or Pharisaic austerity in his piety. Cheerfulness without levity, even sportiveness without rudeness or scandal, marked his whole intercourse with me.

One most intimate with him remarks: "I never knew any one who so delighted in the services of the sanctuary. His whole mind and soul were occupied in the services, his voice always raised in the anthems of praise, his face radiant with heavenly joy, almost as beautiful as it now doubtless appears among those who have washed their robes in the blood of the Lamb."

He never indulged nor countenanced the carping criticism that censoriously or wittily reviews the sermons of the humblest and least cultivated of the ministers of the Word, but was accustomed to say that the Christian might find food for the soul in evangelical discourses that had little intellectual merit, and that it grieved him to listen to cynical comments on the discourses of godly, though humble men, whose whole souls and lives were devoted to the service of God and their fellow-men.

Professor Coleman was eminently a benevolent man, accustomed to "do good by stealth," unostentatiously to distribute his charities, and though known as a liberal contributor to all practical benevolences, yet often dispensing blessings without letting his right hand know what his left hand did.

He shrunk from any ostentation of benevolence, and sometimes said, in domestic confidence, that he gave less in public subscriptions than his heart dictated, lest it should be thought that he gave for the sake of having it known, or from impulsive emulation of others of larger means. Strictly, sensitively conscientious, he sought ever to know what duty to God and man required of him, and he was so jealous of his reputation as a man of nicest sense of honor, and as an upright Christian, that he dreaded lest a suspicion should rest upon any mind that he was capable of neglecting the slightest obligation.

In 1859 Mr. Coleman was elected Professor of the Latin language and literature in the University of

Virginia, as successor to the erudite and lamented Dr. Gessner Harrison. Thus, at the early age of thirty-four years, he had reached the highest position attainable in his profession. For this post he proved himself to be admirably fitted. "Here," says one capable of forming a judicious opinion, "he had gained the proper field, here his desire for usefulness had scope in which to display itself, and here, while following his honorable and useful career, he might have garnered for posterity the golden fruit of his ripe scholarship and experience. His short tenure of the position gave full promise of all."

When this opening presented itself, his mind was greatly exercised as to the propriety of the change. He thought over it long and earnestly, and in fervent prayer sought for counsel and direction from his Heavenly Father. When he had decided the question, he remarked: "The world may think I am prompted by ambition, yet I feel assured I have higher motives. I desire not only the improvement of the talents God has given me, small as they are, but I long for more time to devote to my spiritual improvement." He said that his mind seemed petrifying under the perpetual monotonous round, and for the sake of more leisure and better opportunities for intellectual and spiritual culture, he was willing to sacrifice considerable pecuniary advantages in assuming the new position.

During his first year at the University the labor required of him by the new and unaccustomed duties were so oppressively burdensome that his health became in a few months seriously impaired, and towards the close of the session, under their augmented pressure, his friends trembled lest mind and body should give way under the perpetual strain. Yet no entreaties could induce him to relax his exertions, or to spare himself the slightest details of his duties. He won the confidence and admiration of students and

associate professors, and proved himself, by his
thorough scholarship, his entire familiarity with the
subjects he taught, his felicitous methods of impart-
ing instruction, his promptness, industry and zeal, to
be "the right man in the right place."

During the second session he was relieved of much
of the drudgery of the work by the appointment of
an assistant, and he was able to devote some leisure
hours to the prosecution of higher studies than those
directly associated with his Professorship. This he
had often longed for, and had been hitherto too busy
to attempt. He now prosecuted the study of the
German language and entered upon a course of reading in general literature.

But most of all he delighted in his increased religious privileges. He was as regular as the minister
in his visits to the house of God, punctual in his at-
tendance upon the chapel services, invariably at the
prayer meetings of the students, where his voice was
always heard mingling in the songs of Zion, and often
in leading the devotions of the pious in fervent
prayer, with a sweetness and fervency that left
salutary and favorable impressions on the hearts of
many.

The Sabbath school of colored children and adults
was without a superintendent. He was solicited to
take the office. Reluctantly and from a mere sense
of duty he consented, fearing that it might prove
irksome and interfere with more congenial services.
But soon his heart became interested in the work,
and his higher and most pleasing duties were not
more faithfully performed. "Often," says his devoted wife, "have I seen him leave a circle of students, all fascinated by his conversation, and, with
his little daughter by the hand, hasten to this work
of the Sabbath evening; a work that in a little
while he really enjoyed, hoping, as he said, that he
was doing good. And that sweet little one, after

joyously joining in with the negro children in their simple and spiritual songs, unconscious of what sort of service honored her father most, as if announcing his highest dignity, would gleefully report to all comers, "My Pa is superintendent of the black Sunday school."

His Sabbath days were not spent in indolent loitering. The early hours were passed in private devotion and in religious exercises with the gathered family. A season was devoted to the careful study, not cursory perusal, of the word of God. He said, "It ruins the Epistles to read them in a broken manner, by single or scattered chapters." Dr. McGuffy's lectures on the Psalms; the Professors' Bible class, organized at his instance and conducted by the chaplain; the public services of the sanctuary; the colored Sabbath school; then public service again at night, filled up the hours of the holy day. And in the intervals he cordially received such students as chose to come at his house, quieting his wife's scruples concerning receiving company upon the Lord's day by saying that he had but little opportunity for exerting religious influence over the young men, and as Sunday was their only leisure day, he was glad to welcome some of them under his roof. His brilliant conversational talent, his winning social spirit, his uniform gentleness and kindness of manner, attracted even strangers within his sphere, and then fastened them as personal friends.

John R. Thompson, Esq., has kindly furnished the following sketch of Professor Coleman, which may here be appropriately introduced :

"It was my happy fortune to know Lewis Minor Coleman well during a period of several years, which commenced with his University life and ended only with his martyrdom in the cause of his country, and this intimacy but tended to strengthen the affection I felt for him at college, and to enhance the admiration which was there excited by his intellectual endowments. Few, very few men, redeem in later years the promise they may have given in the curriculum of the University. But it was a characteristic of Coleman that he made every acquisition the stepping stone to something yet higher and nobler beyond, and his under-graduate honors had no value in his eyes other than as associated with those instructions which enabled him to reach forward to a still more thorough and exhaustive knowledge.

His gifts were rich and varied. He had a keen perception of the ludicrous and a lively enjoyment of mirthful sallies, and his conversation was at times lighted up by flashes of wit, but the laughter he excited was always chaste, and he never sacrificed the feelings of others to a *bon mot*. There was too much charity and kindness in his disposition for this, and his ambition soared far above the reputation of a brilliant conversationalist. So much heart had he, indeed, that humor predominated largely over wit,— a quiet, gentle humor like that of Charles Lamb, that broke out in sunny gleams over the barrenest topics. He had also a delicate sense of the beautiful in art, in literature and in the natural world. He was an industrious reader, and his mind drew to itself all that was true and elevated and wholesome in whatever he read, rejecting the false and the noxious, as the bee draws honey even from poisonous flowers; and a memory singularly retentive, coming just here to his aid, he kept in his mental warehouse, as weapons are kept in an armory, all the treasures of poetry and philosophy ready for instant use. All wild and romantic scenery he greatly enjoyed. I recollect to have met him once, just after his return from a trip up the Saguenay in Canada East, and his descriptions of what he had seeen were full of an unstudied grace and eloquence such as is rarely found in books of travel.

In the line of usefulness he had marked out for himself he reached the highest possible eminence, and deserves as a teacher to be ranked with Dr. Arnold, of Rugby, whom it was said, he had made his model. I have been with him at Hanover Academy, both in his hours of teaching and his hours of play, and seen him among his pupils, beloved, never feared, always respected, the master of their confidence and their affections. His sympathies were with them in the play-ground and in the recitation room. His temper was the sweetest, and his discipline at once the most kindly and unbending of any Dominie that ever sat in magisterial authority over a school-room. The fruits of his system of instruction had already manifested themselves before his death in a higher standard of academical training throughout Virginia.

As a private gentleman, as the warmly attached friend, the delightful companion, the sincere, humble Christian, the patriot, carrying his life in his hand when his country called for it, I need not speak of him. I cannot think of his early death, a sacrifice to this war, without recalling the remarkable words of Lord Clarendon in concluding his lofty eulogy on Lucius Carey, Lord Falkland, wherein the historian speaks of that lamented nobleman as 'having so much despatched the business of life, that the oldest rarely attained to that immense knowledge, and the youngest enter not into the world with more innocency,' and we may add, slightly varying the language of the sentence, that 'whoso leads such a life need not care in what manner or at what age it be taken from him.'"

The portentous clouds threatening the rushing tempest of war threw their gloomy shadows over these serene and happy scenes. Professor Coleman promptly settled for himself the course to be pursued in the issues that were forced upon us. "He believed in the sovereignty of his native State; he believed that the rights and privileges guarantied to us in the Constitution had been disregarded by our Northern foes; and he earnestly believed that nothing remained for the South but the exercise of the right of secession or revolution. Virginia was invaded; his allegiance was due to Virginia, and was only subordinate to his allegiance to his God. God and the State alike demanded that Virginia's sons should defend her borders." He deemed it his duty to remain at his post in the University until the close of the session. Even under the impulses of his fervent patriotism, he would not abandon duties to which he considered himself pledged. With the close of the term he tendered his resignation to the Board of Visitors. The Board refused to accept it, keeping the place vacant for his return at the termination of the war.

When the early expedition to Harper's Ferry was determined on, many of the students at the University volunteered for that enterprise. A younger brother asked Professor Coleman's advice concerning his joining the company. "It is your duty, Malcolm," said he, "to decide for yourself." Shortly after his decision was made, he said to his wife: "Malcolm has determined to go, and I am much pleased. I wanted him to go, but felt that I ought not to influence him."

He remained with the gathering students at the depot till a late hour, encouraging and cheering them until the cars bore them away. Then throwing himself upon his sleepless bed, he exclaimed: "I am so sorry I did not make a speech to those noble boys. The poor fellows called me out too. Some of them I may never see again, and, upon the verge of so important a step, I failed to urge upon them the performance of their whole duty in this matter, and especially to remind them of their accountability to God. How I regret that I did not speak to them."

Mr. Coleman loved his profession. He was admirably fitted for it. He had reached the most prominent position to which intellectual ambition can aspire in this country, for there is no literary height to which any man can climb from a Professorship in the University of Virginia. He is there upon the summit of his profession—there are no peaks above.

On the other hand, he had no predilection, no training, no taste for a soldier's life, no aspirations for military renown. Personally such a life was intensely distasteful. He anticipated the service with shrinking repugnance. It severed him from his dear family. It broke up his loved habits of study. It took him from his books which were his delight. It dispelled the serenity and calm in which he found his highest enjoyment.

Nor was there any compulsion to drive him to the army. He was beyond the reach of all conscription laws. He was specially exempted. His friends urged upon him the importance of his position in the University. Some of the Faculty protested against his resignation. Many argued with him that he could do more good to the country by remaining to aid in the education of the neglected youth. Every dissuasive that affection and prudence could suggest were employed to turn him from his purpose.

But in this, as in everything else, he was earnestly conscientious. He felt sad because of the necessity, yet, impelled by a fervent patriotism, he would not shrink from the duty which he felt he owed to his country.

A cherished friend has well said: " In the hour of his country's trial, when the call was made for her children, he relinquished his cherished pursuits, his high and well-merited position, fortune, comfort, home, all—and at last, even life itself—and freely chose to stand where his unfailing perception of the right pointed him, by his country's standard in the battle for freedom. Few, even in these days of sacrifice, have placed a richer gift on the altar of liberty."

Immediately after the first battle of Manassas, he returned to his native county, enlisted in the service and received authority to raise an artillery company. Some discouraged the attempt by representing that most, who could be induced to volunteer, had already entered the army—that attempts of a similar kind had been made and failed. But he listened to no discouragements, and entered upon the work with characteristic energy. He appointed meetings and made speeches which roused the patriotic ardor of the people like a trumpet blast. His graphic pictures of the perils of the country, and of the methods by which it might be delivered from oppression, and rendered free and prosperous, often drew tears from eyes unaccustomed to weep.

In beating up recruits, he visited the house of a poor, aged woman, who resided on his farm, enquiring after her son. The son was already in the service. In speaking of his visit, the old lady said— 'Captain Coleman looked about and found my Bible; he read to me, and then we knelt down, nobody but him and me, and such a beautiful prayer as he offered I never heard in all my life. Just to think! he should take so much interest in a poor old woman like me! He certainly must be the best man in the world."

Such incidents illustrate the predominating spiritual-mindedness of the man.

By such influences and energies a very large company was speedily recruited which was mustered into service, under Mr. Coleman as Captain, in August, 1861.

He now devoted himself with characteristic energy and perseverance to the acquisition of the military knowledge necessary for his position. He soon learned all that the books could teach him. I visited him in camp on one occasion, by his invitation, to preach for his company, and found him drawn up in line, with a few of his brother officers, receiving instructions in practical sword exercises. He omitted nothing that promised to promote his intelligence and efficiency as an officer. The friend to whom I am indebted for so much that is interesting in this sketch says: "By study and continued practice, he made himself one of the best artillery officers in the service, and his company also became one of the most thoroughly drilled and efficient in the army. Here, again, his power in controlling men was strikingly exhibited. Strict in discipline and in every requirement of duty, he was just and impartial, sedulous to supply all the wants of his men, furnishing them, when necessary, with shoes and clothing from his own purse, nursing them personally when sick—kind and affable at all times. He set the example of duty himself and required all to come up to the standard." He soon gained the confidence and affection of his men. He made them feel that he relied upon them, and that they might depend upon him.

Captain Dance, of Powhatan, was preparing a company at the same time and place, for the field, and was consequently thrown into close intercourse with Captain Coleman. He says: "I was struck, upon my first acquaintance with him, with his genial temperament and fine social qualities, rendering him at all times a most agreeable companion; but I soon learned to admire still more his untiring energy, perseverance and industry, as exhibited in his endeavors to equip and drill his company, and perfect himself and them in the necessary knowledge of tactics and military science. The first attempts at drilling his company excited a smile among those who had longer experience; but in a very short time his company was well drilled. His was a spirit never satisfied with mediocrity. Whatever he undertook he desired to do well and he always succeeded. Although his company was mustered in after mine," continues Captain Dance, " yet he succeeded in getting all ready and starting before me."

In this relation, too, he manifested an earnest, practical Christian spirit. He provided, so far as possible, for the religious instruction and culture of his men. Upon every suitable opportunity he solicited ministers of the gospel to preach for them. He conversed with them personally concerning their need of piety toward God, and trust in Him as a preparation for the trials of life and for death.

Regularly, when the bugle sounded the reveille, in early dawning, and the tattoo in the evening, he was among the first to come from his tent, and taking his position in front of the line with uncovered head and raised hands, like a father at his family altar, he solemnly and in clear tones, that reached the extremity of the line, implored the favor and blessing of Almighty God upon his men. This, it is true, was not required by the regulations. It was seen and felt to be the sincere and voluntary devotion of a pious heart.

In speaking of these religious exercises held at the head of his company, Captain Kirkpatrick characterizes them as " those direct, earnest, deeply fervent prayers for which he was remarkable," and then says : "indeed, he had to a degree that few have, the real gift of prayer. I shall never forget the prayer he offered on the sad and memorable Sabbath morning when we commenced our retreat from Centreville. His heart was very tender and very full, and it seemed to unburden itself into the sympathizing ear of that Saviour, who is God over all, blessed forever, and who yearns over all His troubled children with such unspeakable tenderness."

"I have listened on some of these occasions," says another brother officer, "when his prayers, giving evidence of a highly cultivated intellect, yet marked by deep humility and fervent sincerity, left the impression that he would have been a most efficient minister of the gospel, had he been called to that holy office."

Another says : "Though I always had a high opinion of his power and felicity of expression, yet in these *extempore* prayers, I was frequently struck with the force and eloquence, and always with the earnestness and fervor of his petitions."

Oh! if such concern were generally exhibited by officers, nominally pious, for the higher, the spiritual welfare of their men, how much more easily would they be controlled; how effectively restrained from wrong and encouraged in right. Do such exhibitions of solicitous piety weaken discipline? Rather do they strengthen it, by superadding a sense of obligation to the army regulations. Do they diminish courage? He is the bravest fighter, other things being equal, who has the firmest trust in God. Even Infidelity can see that such a spirit must make heroes of an army.

Under such influences and energies, it is not wonderful that his company became one of the best disciplined and most efficient in the service. At a trial of skill between several rival companies, soon after reaching Manassas, his command was pronounced, by competent judges, to be the second if not the best in the corps.

Especially was this company distinguished at the bloody battle of Sharpsburg, where in the heat of the conflict, and amid severe suffering, it gallantly maintained its position, and nobly aided in the defeat of the enemy

The day before his company was ordered to the field his aged grandmother visited him at Richmond. They were together at the residence of a mutual friend. Captain Coleman went into her room just before she retired and kneeling at the dear old lady's feet, said : "Grandma I shall leave in the morning before you are up, and I may never see you again in this world, for this is a serious, earnest work which I have undertaken, and I want you to bless your child before he parts from you." And placing the hand of this aged saint upon his head, he received from her, who for more than fifty years has been a bright and shining light in the Church of God, the patriarchal blessing. In imitating this beautiful ancient and oriental custom, is evinced Mr. Coleman's familiarity and reverence for the old Bible. When a child of six years old, for so early he could read readily, that old grandmother would spread the Family Bible upon a chair, and Lewis, drawing his little stool before it, would sit and pore over its narratives for hours together. It was not unnatural, then, that the association of childhood strengthened in youth and manhood ; that his whole spirit, imbued with the fitness and beauty of the old customs, should have led him to feel " that his heart would be lightened and encouraged in the discharge of a sacred though dangerous duty by receiving from the eldest of the family" the formal patriarchal blessing.

His company was ordered to Manassas and formed a part of General Pendleton's Reserve Corps of Artillery. Time will not permit us to do more than follow the track of the company in the retreat from Manassas, the march to Yorktown and the withdrawal from the Peninsula, the battles around Richmond and the marches to the Rappahannock and to Maryland, in all which it honorably participated.

At the reorganization of the army in 1862, Captain Coleman was appointed Major of artillery and

soon after was elected Lieutenant Colonel of the first
regiment of Virginia artillery

Colonel Coleman was always to be found in his
place, never absenting himself from the post of duty
except from necessity, and once, for several weeks,
from sickness.

During the battles around Richmond he was, by a
mistake of position, for a short time in the hands of
the enemy. But he managed, by his coolness and
presence of mind, to extricate himself. Speaking of
the terrible storm of battle, he said, that while beyond
conception it was awful, yet a relying trust in God
gave him perfect confidence and peace. One of his
fellow officers remarked that the earnestness and sincerity of his ejaculatory prayers upon the battle field,
convinced him "that the soul of Colonel Coleman was
always fixed upon the one sure hope and source of
strength."

"We were drawn up in line of battle," says Captain Kirkpatrick, " on the eastern bank of the Chick-
ahominy, with the advancing enemy in front, on a
Sabbath morning in April or May, 1862. Captain
Coleman approached where I was lying, took from my
hands the Bible I had been reading and turning to
the 84th Psalm, read it and commented upon its
beautiful verses. I can now recall the earnest longing tones, in which he repeated, 'How amiable are Thy
tabernacles, Oh! Lord of Hosts! My soul longeth,
yea, even fainteth for the courts of the Lord; my
heart and my flesh crieth out for the living God!' He
drew a parallel between David's condition when he
composed that Psalm, and ours as we had been driven
by our enemies, and spoke of the wonderful adapted-
ness of God's word, when even such circumstances,
as those around us, only the more forcibly impressed
its truths and beauties upon the soul. He then went
on to speak in glowing words, of the sweet privileges of God's House, the solemn assemblies of His

saints, their blissful communion with Him in all the ordinances of His worship. The impression made upon me by that reading and those running comments will never be effaced from my memory, and while my soul retains its powers, the 84th Psalm will be associated in my mind, with Lewis Minor Coleman and that beautiful but anxious Sabbath morning."

He was prevented by severe illness from accompanying the army into Maryland in 1862. Even then his active spirit chafed under the necessary restraint. He requested a brother officer to send for him if there was any prospect of a battle. In the dead hour of night he heard a rap at the door. "Tis a message for me," said he, "and I must go." Said his wife, "you cannot go; you have not strength to walk across the room." "No matter," he replied, "I will go; God will give me strength." Fortunately, the message related to some other matter.

A short time before the battle of Fredericksburg he resumed his command. Three days before that fatal battle, while riding with a friend towards Port Royal, his friend remarked, "In the seven days fight around Richmond I fought literally over my father's grave; my gun being but a few yards from it. If I should fall in this war, I should prefer to fall upon such, to me, sacred ground." Colonel Coleman replied, "If I am killed in this war I should prefer to fall here, for hard by my father lies buried." Three days after, not far distant, he received his mortal wound.

I am permitted to make a few extracts from letters written during his services in the army, which allow us a glance into his inner life, and reveal to us a little of his pure and loving heart.

In immediate expectation of a battle near Yorktown, April 27th, 1862. He thus writes:

"DEAREST MOTHER: I have a little time this Sabbath afternoon, and will write a few lines to tell you how strongly, at this last moment, when no one knows what an hour may bring forth, the thought of all the love and tenderness and fostering care bestowed in my childhood, comes over your loving son. If I have ever caused you needless trouble, let me now ask your forgiveness. All that I am, all the happiness I have ever enjoyed, is, I believe, due to you, and from you in great measure, under Providence, comes my hope of immortal life. I thank God that I can and do love, from my heart of hearts, all who are near to me, father, mother, grandma, (God bless her,) brothers, sisters, wife, children, all. * * *

"I pray and hope that I may be spared to see you all in peace and happiness again. No one can tell what his fate may be in the bloody struggle which impends, and if I fall, I want you all to know how dearly I love you, and to know further that my only hope and confidence is in God through Jesus Christ our Lord."

In writing of his beloved wife, who while visiting her sick father, had been surprised and detained within the enemy's lines, and separated from her children, after expressing his pain and regret he says : "But it was right for her to go and see her dying father, notwithstanding the suffering it involves. Suffering encountered in the path of duty can never do harm."

Upon the death of the youngest brother of the family he thus writes, just a month before his own death summons:

"MY DEAREST MOTHER:—It is with heartfelt anguish that I have just learned of dear Willie's death. I know your heart is bowed down with grief at the loss of your youngest born—so sweet, so gentle, so lovely in all respects. I always regarded him as the lamb of the flock. * * * Can you not, my dear mother, in this dark hour, put your whole trust and confidence in Our Heavenly Father, who doeth all things well. God grant that we may all strive to be little children, as our dear Willie was."

After speaking of the grief of two young brothers, who were with him in the service, he adds,

"I trust that this great affliction, which for the present seemeth so very grievous, may bring to them a far more exceeding and eternal weight of glory. I trust, too, that I shall be stirred up to be a better guide, both by example and precept, to my two young brothers so strangely associated with me, after so many years of separation."

But I must hasten to the sad close of this sketch. Colonel Coleman was on duty with his regiment at the battle of Fredericksburg, on the 13th of December, under General Jackson, and with unflinching courage, and entire self-possession, maintained his position on that bloody field.

"He might," says Captain Dance, "without any dereliction of duty, have kept out of that battle altogether, for when his regiment was brought up, other artillery had already occupied the position. But he was anxious to render some service, and sought out the General commanding that part of the line, and obtained leave to place some of his guns in position, and two guns of my battery were all he could find room for, and it was at one of these that he received the wound which finally proved mortal. His horse had been killed, and though on foot and wounded, he still insisted upon remaining on the ground, and even offered his assistance in filling up a ditch, that my guns might be carried over to advance on the enemy."

Late in the day he was struck by a ball in the leg, just below the knee. He deemed the wound a slight one, and, as we have seen, refused to leave the field, until by increasing faintness he was compelled to do so, but not until the victory had been decided for our arms. When his wound was dressed, he

playfully remarked that it would be a "good furlough"
for awhile. He was borne to the house of Mr. Yerby
in Spotsylvania county. Here, when found by his
uncle, Rev. James D. Coleman, he was surrounded
by the wounded and dying, to whom in his benevolent self-forgetfulness, he was striving to administer
such aid and consolation as was in his power. He
spoke more of his suffering comrades than of himself, and especially expressed his sympathy and sor-
row for a terribly mutilated young officer, who was
lying by his side. He was removed to Edge Hill,
Caroline county, the residence of his brother-in-law,
Mr. Samuel Schooler. Soon his wound assumed a
threatening and dangerous character. Virulent erysipelas supervened, and he suffered intense agony.
By profuse discharges from his wound, and by con-
stant severe pain, his frame became emaciated and
reduced to little more than a skeleton. Every attention which the skill of physicians and the affectionate care and nursing of the assembled family
could render, could only retard, but could not over-
come the steady approaches of coming death. His
friends were unwilling to believe, that one for whom
they so ministered, for whose recovery they so fer-
vently prayed, upon whose continued life so many
hopes and interests were depending, must be taken
from them. But the gravest fears were soon excited,
and before long Colonel Coleman himself began to
anticipate his speedy departure from earth. He endured with marvelous patience and uncomplaining
cheerfulness the most excruciating agonies of body.
His faith in the rectitude and benevolence of his covenant God, never wavered, rather steadily increased
as death approached nearer and still nearer. And
now the beautiful light of his pious spirit, like the
glories of a clear autumn sunset, illumed the chamber in which he was gasping away his life, and
lighted up, with sweet resignation and hope, the

hearts of his lamenting kindred. In the early stages of his disease he hoped—expected to recover. He had much for which to live, and few men could better enjoy or adorn life, or render it more useful than he. He now decided, what before he had often pondered, that with recovered health, he would devote his life and talents to the more direct service of God, in the work of the gospel ministry. "At the close of the war," said he, "more than ever will laborers be needed to reap in the harvest field of the gospel. I may do some good in that sphere of labor." But a higher ministry, in a brighter sphere, had been appointed for him. "I hope I shall live," said he to a friend, "I think I can do good—be of some use; but God knows best and His will be done." In the solitary night, when a troubled sleep could be induced only by means of powerful opiates, his mind would wander fitfully over the scenes of the past. Now he would imagine himself in presence of a class of pupils teaching, and he would recite rapidly in Latin and French, and then he seemed at the head of his company in the battle, and uttered the stern word of command. Then the names of distant friends, as in cheerful and social converse, passed his lips; then the dear names of "wife," "mother," "child," in loving murmurs proved whither his restless thoughts were turning, and always the devotional ejaculation, of praise to God, and of fervent prayer for grace and strength, would mingle with his wildest wanderings.

In one of these restless hours, shortly before he died, he roused himself and turning to his brother said: "Malcolm, did I die as a Christian soldier ought to die?"—then entirely recovering consciousness, he smiled and said, "I thought I had died on the battle-field."

For ninety-eight weary days, he endured physical agonies, relieved by only occasional respites from pain, such as probably few men have ever been called

4

to bear. The incurable erysipelas, the inflammation involving the whole limb, and extending by sympathy to his whole frame, the frequent incisions and probings, the drain from incessant suppuration, the inaccessible ulcers originating in his changeless position on the couch, all combined to produce excruciating pain. Yet all was borne with a patience, resignation, even cheerfulness, that has, perhaps, never been surpassed. When convinced that there was no rational hope of his recovery, he fixed the eye of his faith steadily upon the bright home in heaven, and seeming to enter already into communion with the beloved ones who had gone before, looked beyond the interval over which he must pass, and lived as though already in the light of his Redeemer's glory. He was more than patient, he was exultant, at times enraptured.

Referring to the fact that he was in the neighborhood where much of his youth had been spent, he said, " Here were most of the sins of my early life committed, and here do I come to die, and to find them all forgiven through the mercy and love of Jesus."

" Why, it is but a short trip," said he to his weeping friends. " It is only taking a little journey, and then safe and happy forever. It is but a trip, we shall all meet again soon, and I want to start and be with Christ."

" I had hoped," said he, " to do good, living, as a minister of the gospel, but perhaps God will make my death a ministry for the conversion of those dear ones who are yet out of Christ. I may do more good by dying than by living." These hopes have not been in vain. One of his brothers has already united with the church of Christ. Another dear friend to whom he had appealed in a former serious illness, and to whom, later, he sent this message : "Tell Charles M——— that I once before knocked at the door of his heart, and that he must strive to meet me in heaven," writes me, "his warning, from the death-bed, I trust has not been in vain. I feel that, under God, I now have a hope of a better life." He called all the household, even the servants, to his bed-side, and tenderly gave them his dying counsels, and bade them loving farewells. He asked them what messages he should bear for them to the ransomed loved ones who had gone before.

Referring to the recent death of his youngest brother, he said, with a sweet smile, to his brother, Dr. Coleman, "Dear little Willie! I shall be more fortunate than you were, Robert, you went to Lexington to see him and were disappointed, but I shall not be disappointed. I shall certainly see him."

Turning to his beloved wife, who had been an unwearied watcher and ministrant during his lingering illness, says Rev. Mr. Coleman, " he pronounced upon her character and life a most tender and beautiful eulogy, and in words that seemed to gush from the depths of his soul, praised, and thanked, and blessed her, for the happiness and joy which her love had brought to his heart and life."

He charged those who ministered to him with pious messages to the absent. " Tell General Jackson and General Lee," said he, " they know how Christian soldiers can fight, and I wish they could see now how a Christian soldier can die."

In communicating this message to General Jackson, Dr. Coleman wrote, " I doubt not, General, that the intimate acquaintance with yourself which my brother desired on earth, will be vouchsafed to him in heaven, and that when your career of usefulness here is ended, 'in the green pastures and beside the still waters' of a brighter sphere, you and he will meet in sweet communion and. fellowship, and that your earthly acquaintance will be purified and perfected into an eternal friendship."

General Jackson's response was characteristic. He writes :

" Had your brother lived, it was my purpose to become better acquainted with him. I saw much less of him than I desired. I look beyond this life to an existence where I hope to know him better.

"Very truly, your friend,

"T. J JACKSON."

When scarcely five weeks had passed, these anticipations were realized, and these sainted spirits met, where no sounds nor perils of war will evermore disturb the holy repose and bliss of their communion.

As Arnold had been his model as a teacher, so Havelock was his model as a Christian soldier. And almost the words of Havelock were those which he transmitted in this dying message to his own beloved Generals.

Once only when writhing in agony intense, did his faith for a brief space seem to fail, and he expressed a dread that God's face was hid from him. A few days after, he recalled this expression of doubt to mind and said : " Doctor, you remember I said I did not feel God's presence with me. I could not hear the rustling of the angels' pinions. Now I *know* that he is near me, and I feel the breath of the angels' wings."

He exacted from his younger brother, Dr. Malcolm Fleming, who watched constantly at his bedside, a promise that he would let him know when his end was approaching. When his feeble, sinking pulse indicated the speedy termination of his sufferings, Malcolm said to him, with throbbing heart and streaming eyes, "Brother Lewis, you remember my promise." "Yes, Malcolm ; do you think I am dying ?" He could only bow his head in answer. Immediately, with as much composure as he had ever given a lecture to a class, he dictated his last will and then fell asleep as calmly as in childhood. When he awoke he expressed surprise that he still lived. He had fallen asleep amid the farewells of loving lips and the suppressed wailings of bleeding hearts. He had hoped to waken in heaven. "Come, Lord Jesus, come quickly, O come quickly," was his frequent prayer. He was asked "would you not prefer to stay with us?" "No! no!" he replied, "'I prefer to go." They sang, at his request, such hymns as—

> "Jesus, and shall it ever be,
> A mortal man ashamed of Thee."

And

> "How firm a foundation, ye saints of the Lord,
> Is laid for your faith in His excellent Word."

And in feeble tones, he joined in the sacred songs. Late in the night he asked them to sing the hymn commencing—"Jesus, I love Thy charming name," and the last verse he sung with them in faltering, dying tones—

> "I'll speak the honors of Thy name
> With my last laboring breath—
> And dying, clasp Thee in my arms,
> The antidote of Death."

Some said to him, "You will soon be in Heaven; are you willing to go?" "Perfectly willing; Certainly I am." They were his last words, and, soon, in the early dawn of the morning, on the 21st of March, 1863, he fell asleep in Jesus.

When the summons of death comes to us, may we each be ready to say—"Perfectly willing; Certainly I am."

Young Men! we have thus presented for your contemplation, an imperfect surview of the life of a Christian scholar and soldier. The extraordinary deeds of some world-worshipped hero or fabulous demigod might, perhaps, have better amused or entertained the multitude. But such a sketch as this cannot fail to be more useful, in so far as it is practical and imitable. Here are excellencies you may attain, a character you may emulate, a life you may copy.

"If no faults shade the picture," to quote the beautiful sentiment of Rev. Dr. Hoge, in speaking of another of Virginia's noble sons fallen in battle, "it is not because I have hidden them from my readers, but because grace has hidden them from me."

It may be true that Colonel Coleman's natural mental endowments, his original physical capabilities were of a higher order, than God has given to most. But as a practical life I have endeavored to sketch one that is plainly imitable.

Perhaps the most prominent characteristic of his moral nature was his conscientiousness. In little matters, as in those more important, he was accustomed to ask, and to act upon the answer, what is duty?

"His conceptions of duty," says Major Venable, one of his earliest and latest friends, "were as true and direct as his performance of it was thorough and exact." This is imitable by all.

Persevering industry, including earnest attention to little things, was another marked feature of Lewis Coleman's life. In his studies, earlier and later, in all the practical routine of daily requirements, in the study and lecture-room, on the farm and in the camp, whatever service devolved upon him, was promptly performed. He seldom had arrearages of business to bring up. He pushed his work steadily before him, rarely needing to drag it along after its appropriate hours. Such an example may be wisely copied.

He was uniformly cheerful and social. He always had a pleasant word for all he met, even for servants. His lively wit, without a shade of malice or ill-nature, his honest, ringing laugh, the wonderful sprightliness, felicity and tact of his ordinary conversation, drawing as from a perennial spring, sparkling rills of facts fancies and illustrations, made him a most genial and instructive companion

He evinced in all his life the most unselfish benevolence of spirit. He sought to promote the happiness of others rather than his own. He lived for others rather than for himself. No friend ever asked him for a favor, who did not meet a cheerful and ready response, if the bestowment was within the compass of his means, and the approval of his conscience.

And for the happiness and welfare of the loved ones of his own family circle, no sacrifice was deemed too severe. There seemed only one earthly love that could surpass that of mother, father, brothers, sisters, wife and children for him, and that was his love for them.

And this trait of heart, too, is imitable.

Throwing its soft light over all these excellencies was his beautiful humility. He rarely made himself, or any thing that he did, the theme of conversation. " He was a man of few professions," says Major Venable, " and his Christianity found more expression in action than words, yet it was not difficult to read the clear simplicity of his life and character."

He never seemed himself aware that there was anything especially meritorious or unusual in his sweet, genial, benevolent life. He never seemed conscious, even upon his death-bed, that he had made any notable sacrifice in resigning his elevated position at the University, for his humble position in the army. He often spoke in desponding tones of the little he had accomplished as a student and a Christian, and ever longed and struggled for higher attainments and higher usefulness.

Is not this temper worthy of imitation ?

The supreme, fostering originating principle of all these excellencies of life and heart was his piety. Early he learned that " beginning of wisdom—the

fear of the Lord." His piety was not the mere color-
ing that ornamented life; it entered into the warp
and woof of his inner nature. He loved God and
lived in daily communion with the Redeemer, and
thus became "a living epistle of Jesus Christ, known
and read of all men."

Have I not well said, that his was an imitable life,
and therefore well worthy of delineation for the study
of young men, who are aiming at something beyond
mere personal, selfish enjoyment—at an honorable,
beneficent life.

One who knew him well and loved him dearly, has
beautifully said: "As the dew, falling silently, re-
freshing and rendering fruitful the earth, and erys-
talizing upon the spires of grass and in the calices of
flowers, crowns, as with diamonds, the brow of morning, so the unostentatious virtues of Lewis Minor
Coleman refreshed the hearts, gladdened and made
fruitful in good deeds the lives of others; and when
the Sun of Righteousness shall arise, those virtues
will shine more resplendantly as gems in that crown
which the Righteous Judge shall give to him on that
day."